The Water Detectives
The Adventures of Mitch and Molly

Karen O'Connor

Illustrated by Len Ebert

PUBLISHING HOUSE

The Adventures of Mitch and Molly

The Green Team
The Water Detectives

For Noah and Johannah
(The real Mitch and Molly in my life)

———— *The Water Detectives* is printed on recycled paper.————

Library of Congress Cataloging-in-Publication Data

O'Connor, Karen, 1938-
    The water detectives: the adventures of Mitch and Molly / Karen O'Connor; illustrated by Len Ebert.
    (God's green earth; bk 2)
    Summary: Five stories in which nine-year-old Mitch and his younger sister Molly find ways to save water, plant trees, and help take care of God's earth.
    ISBN 0-570-04727-7 (alk. paper)
    [1. Conservation of natural resources—Fiction. 2. Environmental protection—Fiction. 3. Brothers and sisters—Fiction.]
I. Ebert, Len., ill. II. Title. III. Series.
PZ7.02224Wat 1993   [E]—dc20 92-24649
                                            CIP

1 2 3 4 5 6 7 8 9 10   02 01 00 99 98 97 96 95 94 93

Contents

Mitch and Molly
Water Detectives

Mitch heard a weird noise. He turned to his sister Molly. Then he looked at their baby-sitter. Jennifer was reading to them in the book corner in Molly's room.

"Jennifer, what's that noise?" asked Mitch. "Molly, can you hear it?"

"I don't hear anything," said Molly.

"What does it sound like?" asked Jennifer.

"Plop, plop," said Mitch.

"Where is it?" asked Molly.

"I think it's coming from the bathroom," said Mitch.

"Let's take a look," said Jennifer.

Mitch followed Jennifer into the bathroom between his room and Molly's. "I hear it now," said Jennifer.

Mitch watched her check the faucet in his sink. Then she checked the faucet in Molly's sink. "No problem there," she said. "But we're getting closer."

Jennifer opened the bathtub door. "Here it is," she said. "Listen to this. The water is dripping onto your bath mat. That's why it makes a strange sound."

Mitch leaned over the bathtub. He heard the same "plop! plop!" sound again. "That's it," said Mitch.

Jennifer reached in and turned the handles tight. "That will stop that noise," she said. "Somebody forgot to turn the faucet off all the way. If it comes back again, we'll know there's a leak in the pipe." Jennifer turned out the light in the bathroom. Mitch and Molly and Jennifer walked back to Molly's room.

"Say, Mitch, that's pretty good detective

work," said Jennifer. "That makes you an official water detective."

Mitch stopped by the bookcase. "It does? What's a water detective?" asked Mitch.

"Is it somebody who finds a leak?" asked Molly.

"Pretty close," said Jennifer. "That's one thing a water detective does."

"What else?" asked Mitch.

"Sit here," said Jennifer, patting the big red and blue floor pillows. "Water detectives find ways to save water," she said. "Water is one of God's most important gifts."

"We need water to drink and to wash ourselves," said Molly.

"Plants and animals need water too," said Mitch.

"You're both right," said Jennifer. "I learned ways to save water in my ecology class at school."

"What's *ecol* . . . ? What's that word you said?" asked Molly.

"*Ecology* is the study of the environment," said Jennifer.

Mitch could see that Molly still didn't understand. "It's learning about plants and animals and water and recycling and stuff like that," said Mitch. He looked at Jennifer. "I learned about ecology in school too," he said.

"Me too," said Molly. "But our teacher didn't use that word. She calls it 'saving the earth.' "

"It's the same thing," said Jennifer. "Ecology is saving God's green earth. Water savers care about our water. They make sure to turn off the faucets real tight. They only use the water they need. They fix leaky pipes. They pour leftover water on plants instead of throwing it away. And there's lots more they can do."

"I want to be a water detective," said Mitch. "What else should I do?"

Jennifer pulled a book out of her school bag. "Look at this," she said. Mitch watched over Jennifer's shoulder. Molly sat next to her on the pillow. Jennifer read a page in the book. "A leak that fills up a small can in 10 minutes can waste more than 3,000 gallons of water in one year."

"How much water is that?" asked Molly.

"Good question," said Jennifer. "Well, it says here that you would have to drink 65 glasses of water every day for a year to get that much water."

"Wow!" said Mitch. "No one could drink that much."

"And it says that a leaky toilet can waste more than 22,000 gallons of water in one year," said Jennifer. "Can you imagine? That's enough water to take three baths every day."

"I wonder if we have a leaky toilet," asked Mitch.

"Let's find out," said Jennifer. "Do you kids want to do an experiment?"

"Sure," said Mitch. "It's fun being a water detective."

"I want to help too," said Molly.

Jennifer stood up and pulled Molly up by the hand. "All right. Let's get to work," said Jennifer. "Mitch, does your mom have any food coloring?"

"The kind we use to dye Easter eggs?" asked Mitch.

"Yes, that's the kind. Where is it?"

"I know," said Molly. "It's on the second shelf in the pantry."

Jennifer walked down the stairs. Molly ran down. And Mitch slid down the banister.

Jennifer took a bottle of red food coloring from the pantry shelf.

"Here's what we're going to do," she said. "We'll put 12 drops inside each toilet tank. Then we'll wait 15 minutes. Now remember," she said. "You can't use the toilets during this experiment, or it won't work."

"Let's start in our bathroom," said Mitch.

"All right," said Jennifer. "You lead the way."

Jennifer put 12 drops of food coloring in

Mitch and Molly's toilet tank. Next she put some drops in their mom and dad's toilet tank. Then she went downstairs and put 12 drops in the toilet tank in the guest bathroom.

"Mitch, you watch the clock," said Jennifer. "When 15 minutes are up, you look in the toilet bowl in your bathroom. Molly, you look at the one in your mom and dad's bathroom. And I'll check the one in the guest bathroom. Okay? If there's any red water in the bowl, we'll know there's a leak."

"Okay," said Molly. "This is fun."

"Okay," said Mitch. "I'm ready. It's 4:00."

"Good," said Jennifer. "Tell us when it's 4:15."

Mitch watched the big hand on the clock move. At 4:15 he shouted, "It's time. Let's check."

Mitch and Molly ran to the upstairs bathrooms. "I'll meet you down here," said Jennifer.

"Mom and Dad's is okay," shouted Molly.

"The guest bathroom is fine," called Jennifer from the bottom of the stairs.

Mitch slid down the banister. "The water in our toilet turned red."

"That means there's a leak," said Jennifer.

"I heard that *plop! plop!* sound again too," said Mitch.

"That means you have a leak in the bathtub pipes too," said Jennifer.

"We'll have to tell your dad and mom about it when they come home."

"This is fun," said Mitch. "How else can we save water?"

"There are a lot of things you can do. Shall we make a list?" asked Jennifer.

"Good idea," said Mitch. "We could hang it on the bulletin board in the kitchen."

"You could put one in the bathrooms too," said Jennifer.

"I'll get my crayons," said Molly.

"And I've got some poster paper in my closet," said Mitch.

Mitch and Molly and Jennifer sat around

the kitchen table. Jennifer shared some ideas from her ecology book. "You can save water by taking short showers, or by taking a bath with only five inches of water," she said. "You can turn off the water while brushing your teeth. You can keep a pitcher of drinking water in the refrigerator. Then you won't have to run the water till it turns cold."

Jennifer told them some more ideas for saving water in the kitchen and the laundry room. She also told Mitch and Molly how to save water in the yard.

Jennifer finished reading. She turned to Mitch. "Are you ready to make the lists?"

"Sure. Let's hurry so they'll be ready when Mom and Dad come home. You print, Jennifer," said Mitch. "You write faster than me."

"Okay, I'll write the words, you make the numbers," said Jennifer. "And, Molly, would you trace over the numbers with your neon crayons?"

"Okay," said Molly. Mitch watched her

13

dig into her crayon box.

When they finished, Mitch and Molly and Jennifer hung their signs in the bathrooms. A few minutes later Mitch heard a key in the front door lock. He ran into the hall and peered over the railing.

"Mom and Dad are home," he whispered. "Wait till they see our signs."

"And don't forget to tell Daddy about the leaks in our bathroom," said Molly.

"Anybody home?" called Dad.

Mitch and Molly dashed down the stairs.

"Surprise!" shouted Mitch.

"Surprise!" shouted Molly.

"We're here," said Jennifer. "We've been busy. The kids have a lot to share."

"Yeah, Daddy," said Molly. "Jennifer taught us how to be water detectives. A water detective finds leaks and tells people how to save water."

"You'll have to tell us all about it," said Mother. She handed Jennifer her baby-sitting money. "Thanks for taking care of Mitch and Molly," she said. "We'll see you again soon."

"Bye," said Jennifer. "Have fun playing water detectives."

Mitch and Molly waved good-bye.

"Now what's all this about being a water detective?" asked Dad.

"Sounds mysterious to me," said Mother.

Mitch and Molly showed Mother and Dad their lists. Mitch told Dad about the leaks in the bathroom. Then they read the list together.

Save the Earth
Be a Water Detective

1. Fix leaky faucets and toilets.

2. Take five-minute showers, or five-inch baths.

3. Turn off water while brushing your teeth.

4. Put a water-saving shower head in your shower.

---

5. Put a rock or sand bag in toilet tank to save water.

6. Keep a pitcher of cold water in the refrigerator so you don't have to run the tap water.

7. Water the lawn only when it needs it.

8. Turn on the dishwasher only when it's full.

"I'm proud of you both," said Dad. "You sure do take care of God's green earth." Dad put his arm around Mitch and Molly. Then he grabbed Mother by the hand. "Do you think you could teach Mother and me to be water detectives too?"

Mitch laughed. "Sure, Dad. Just follow me."

SOMETHING YOU CAN DO TO SAVE GOD'S GREEN EARTH

Check for leaks in your bathroom and kitchen faucets. Ask an adult to help you check your toilet tanks for leaks, as Mitch and Molly and Jennifer did. If you find a leak, ask your parents to fix it.

Make a list of ways to save water at home. Use Mitch and Molly's list as a guide.

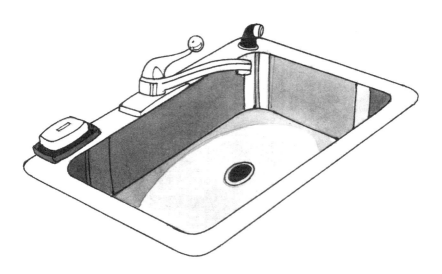

Mitch and Molly
And the Litter Bugs

After school on Wednesday, Mitch ran up to Molly in front of the kindergarten room. "Did you get one of these?" Mitch waved a yellow paper over his sister's head. "Friday is Save-the-Earth Dress-Up Day. That's only two days away."

Molly pulled a yellow paper out of her skirt pocket. "Sure. Here's mine, see?" said Molly, shaking it in Mitch's face. "Dress-Up Day is for everyone in the whole school," she said proudly.

"What are you going to dress like?" asked Mitch.

"Maybe I'll be a bird. I could use the wings

from my angel costume. And Mommy could make me a hat with feathers for the head," said Molly.

"That's a dumb idea. A bird with angel wings. Everyone would laugh at you, Molly."

"Gosh, Mitch, you're not very nice."

Mitch ran down the sidewalk next to the park. "Wait for me," yelled Molly. At the corner Mitch saw a big boy zoom by on his bike. He tossed an empty soda can on the street. He kept on riding. A boy with a neon green shirt rode up behind him. He tossed a potato-chip bag on the grass.

Molly bent down and picked up the can and the bag. "Those boys are litter bugs," she said. "Don't they know every litter bit hurts?"

"Hey, that's funny, Molly. Every litter bit hurts," Mitch repeated. "Where did you hear that?"

"Our teacher told us. She said people who throw trash on the street are litter bugs. And every litter bit hurts. It's on the trash can, see?"

Molly pointed to the big metal container by the swings. She tossed the potato-chip bag and the empty can into it as she walked by.

Mitch read the sign. "EVERY LITTER BIT HURTS." When he looked closer Mitch saw a cartoon drawing of a little bug with a smiling face.

Every piece of litter does hurt God's green earth, thought Mitch. He remembered how nice the park looked after the dump trucks took away the trash. And he thought about how pretty the church grounds looked after the cleanup crew finished their chores. Mitch also remembered Judy, the lifeguard. She had told him how to keep the beach clean for animals and people.

Mitch saw a glass bottle on the grass. He picked it up and threw it in the trash. "Gosh, Molly," said Mitch. "Let's never be litter bugs. Look at those bags and papers on the ground. They're right next to the trash can. Why don't people take one more step and throw their stuff in the can?" Mitch picked up a handful of sand and let it run through his fingers. "The park is a lot prettier when the sand is clean," he said.

"I hate it when people mess up God's earth," said Molly. "Remember what we learned in Sunday school about being a good steward?"

"Sure I do," said Mitch. "We can help keep the earth clean and green." Mitch liked the way the words *clean* and *green* rhymed. Maybe I can think up a poem about God's green earth, thought Mitch. "Let's see. God's earth will stay green, if you help keep it clean." Mitch liked the sound of the words.

"Hey, Molly, I made up a poem. Listen. God's earth will stay green, if you help keep it clean. Isn't that neat?"

"That's neat, Mitch."

Molly skipped ahead, swinging her Cinderella lunch pail. "A steward is some-body who takes care of something, right Mitch?"

"Right."

Mitch thought about the Save-the-Earth Dress-up Day. He wanted to be something special. He wished he could be funny too. But there wasn't anything funny about saving the earth.

Then Mitch got an idea, an idea that was funny and serious and important too. "Hey, Molly, wait up," called Mitch. He ran up to his sister who was hopping over the cracks in the sidewalk.

"Molly, I know what we can be for Save-the-Earth Day. Litter bugs. Isn't that a super idea?"

"Litter bugs? You just said we should never be litter bugs."

"Well, I mean we shouldn't throw our trash on the ground, Molly. But we could dress up like litter bugs for Save-the-Earth Day. And we could carry trash bags. We could tell kids to put their trash in the bags."

"We could put them in our wagon and pull

it with us," said Molly.

"Good idea," said Mitch.

"Let's tell Mommy," said Molly.

Mitch and Molly ran the rest of the way home. Mother was carrying in some firewood as they walked up the driveway. "Mom, Mom, guess what?" Mitch waved the yellow paper. He showed her the note and told her about dress-up day. "We know what we want to be," he said. "Litter bugs."

Mother pushed the front door open with her left elbow. "Here, Mitch, give me a hand, please. This wood is heavy."

Mitch grabbed a log and held the door for his mother. "Litter bugs? Where did you get that idea?" she asked. "It's kind of cute."

"Mitch thought of it," said Molly. "We learned about litter bugs in school. People who throw their trash on the ground are litter bugs. We're going to show the kids how not to be litter bugs, right, Mitch?"

"Right. And Molly got another idea," said

Mitch. He opened the cabinet under the kitchen sink. He pulled out two big trash bags. "We're going to put these in our wagon. We'll make a sign that tells people to put their trash in the bag and not on the ground."

"That sounds great," said Mother. She filled a pot with hot water and turned on the stove. "Daddy won't be home for dinner. He has a meeting after work," she said. "We can eat early, and then work on your costumes."

After dinner, Mitch and Molly washed the dishes. Mother came into the kitchen with a box of material she used for sewing. "I don't see anything here we could use," she said. "What would make a good bug costume?"

"I know," said Molly. "We could wear our green and yellow striped pajamas. Remember the ones Grandma gave us for Christmas?"

"Those baby pajamas? No way," said Mitch. "They're ugly. They have feet in them."

"But the stripes make me think of bugs," said Molly, laughing.

"Now Mitch, they're not that bad," said Mother. "Grandma said she thought they'd keep your feet warm on cold nights. It was a nice idea."

"Grandma asked me if we ever wear them," said Molly. She frowned at Mitch. "I didn't tell her you think they're for babies."

"All right, children," said Mother. "That's enough. They might be just the right thing for your costumes. Molly's right. The long sleeves and feet and the stripes do look like a bug's body. You can wear your green ski hats and black mittens." Mother winked at Mitch and tickled Molly under the chin. "I think you'll be the cutest bugs in town."

Mitch giggled. "We need antennae too," he said.

"Yeah, and we need those skinny things that stick out of their heads," said Molly.

"Molly, that's what antennae are," said Mitch, glaring at his sister.

"Well, I didn't know. Gosh, Mitch you're

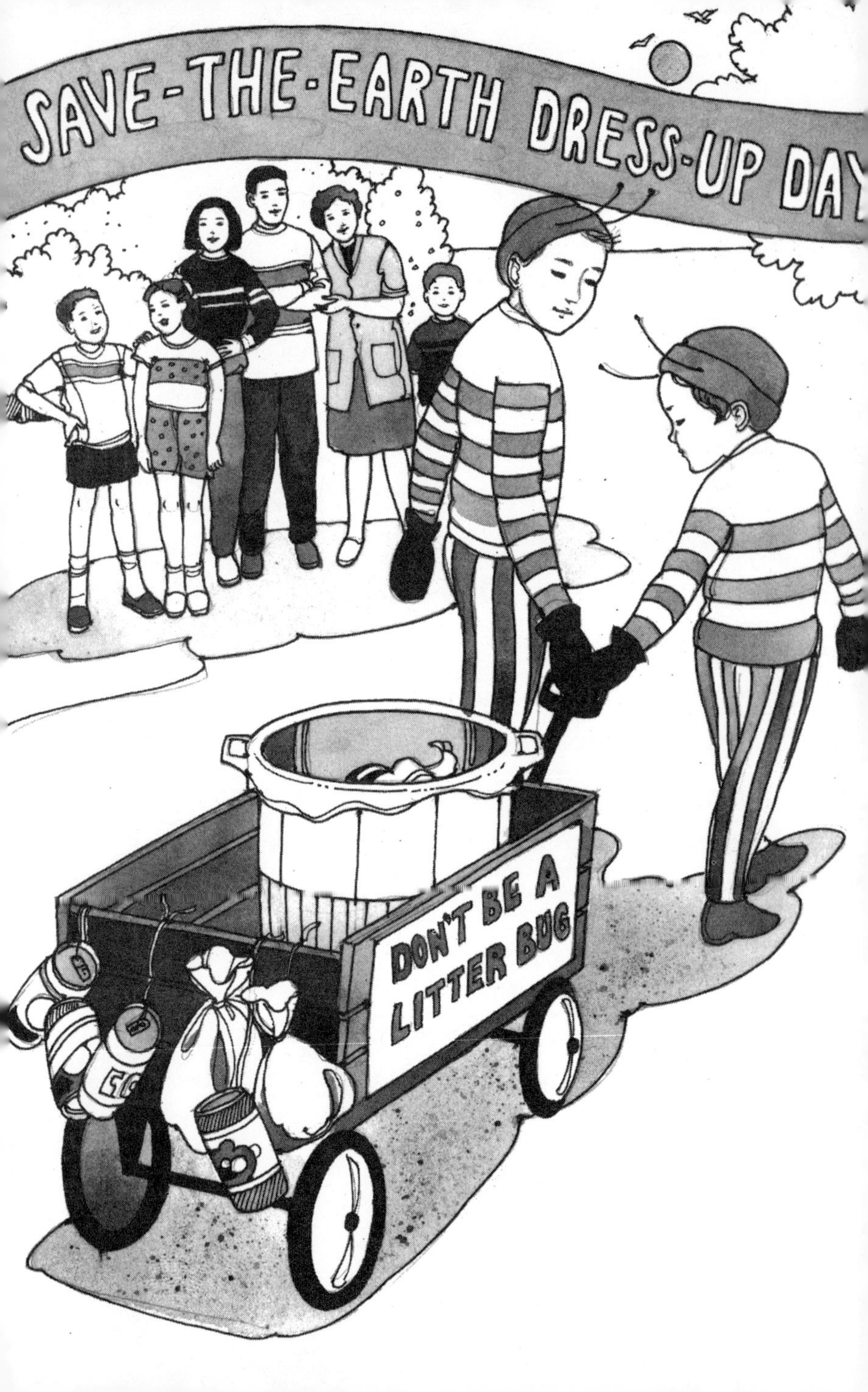
SAVE-THE-EARTH DRESS-UP DAY
DON'T BE A LITTER BUG

not very nice."

Mother walked into the kitchen and came back with some long black fuzzy wire. "These are pipe cleaners," she said. "I've had them in the drawer ever since I taught crafts at Sunday school. They'll work just fine. We can bend them anyway you like."

Mitch and Molly pulled out their green and yellow striped pajamas. Mother ironed them. Then she attached the pipe cleaners to their knit hats. Mitch dug out their mittens from the box in the hall closet.

The next day, after school, Mitch and Molly washed their wagon. They hung aluminum cans and paper bags on the back. Dad came home from work early. He helped Mitch make a sign for each side of the wagon. One said, "Don't Be a Litter Bug." The other one said, "Every Litter Bit Hurts." Molly put a small garbage can with a trash bag in the back of the wagon.

"There you go, kids. You're all set," said Dad. Then he lifted the wagon into Mother's car. Friday morning Dad kissed Mitch and Molly good-bye. "Have fun. I wish I could be there," he said. "But Mother said she'd take some pictures."

Mitch and Molly waved good-bye to Dad. Then they climbed in Mother's car. "I'll be watching for you," said Mother, as she drove up to the school. "I'll stand by the picnic table. Have fun." Mitch and Molly got out of the car. They waved good-bye.

"I'll see you at the parade," Mitch called as Molly ran to her kindergarten room. Her tiny antennae shook as she ran.

At 10:00 the parade started. Mitch found Molly. They lined up with the other students under a big sign. "Save-the-Earth Dress-up Day." They marched around the playground. One boy looked like a tree. He carried a sign that said, "Plant a Tree." A girl in fifth grade was wearing a whale costume. She carried a sign that said, "Save the Whales." Mitch's friend, Matt, had a white T-shirt on and some pants made of old newspapers. The front of his shirt said "Save a Tree. Recycle Your Newspapers."

Mitch saw some of the students looking at the signs on their wagon. Two boys picked up some plastic cups and put them in their trash can. A girl threw some paper in the bag. "Hey, this is neat, Molly. Look how many kids are picking up trash."

"They don't want to be litter bugs," said Molly. "Hey, there's Mommy."

Mitch waved to Mother as they walked by the picnic tables.

"Hi, Mommy," shouted Molly.

Mother waved. "Hi, there, litter bugs. You look great!"

At 11:00 the school bell rang. The parade was over. Mitch listened to the school principal tell all the children what a great job they had done. Then Mitch took the wagon over to Mother. He and Molly waved good-bye.

"I'll see you after school," said Mother.

"Bye, Mitch," Molly called. "It was fun being a litter bug with you."

"Bye, Molly."

That night after supper, Mitch sat down at the table in the family room. He took a sheet of paper and a pencil from his notebook.

"What are you up to?" asked Mother.

"I'm writing a thank-you note to Grandma."

"Did she send you a gift?" asked Mother.

"Yeah! Last Christmas. The green and yellow striped pajamas." Mitch saw his mother smiling behind her hand. Molly giggled. He drew a picture of two litter bugs at the top of the page. Then he wrote Grandma a letter.

> Dear Grandma,
>
> Thanks for the pajamas. I wore them for Save-the-Earth Dress-up Day. Molly and I were litter bugs. I'll send you a picture.
>
> Love,
> Mitch
>
> P.S.
> Here's a poem I wrote.
> Please show it to Grandpa.
> God's earth will stay green,
> If you help keep it clean.

Mitch folded the letter and put it in an envelope. Then he placed it on Dad's dresser so his father could mail it in the morning. Mitch climbed into bed. "Thanks, God," Mitch whispered. "Thanks for dress-up day, and for Grandma and her present, and for Mom and Dad and Molly—and for Your green earth."

SOMETHING YOU CAN DO TO SAVE GOD'S GREEN EARTH

Plan a save-the-earth scavenger hunt for a birthday party. Divide your friends into groups. Make a list of items that can be recycled such as glass jars, cereal boxes, newspapers, and aluminum cans. Have each group go with an adult to neighbors' houses and ask for the items on the list. They must bring back as many things on the list as they can. The first team to return to the starting point with the most items wins the game. Have a prize ready for the winners.

Mitch and Molly, Paper-Savers

Mitch looked at the big gold clock on the wall. It was 10:30. Sunday school was over. Mr. Morgan said a prayer and told the children good-bye. Mitch grabbed his blue sweater from the rack on the wall. Then he waited by the door as his father came to pick him up.

"Dad, Dad, guess what?" shouted Mitch.

"You sound pretty excited," said Dad. "What's happening?"

"We're learning more about God's green earth," said Mitch, waving a note in his hand. "Today our teacher told us about saving paper." Mitch pointed to the words. "Look," he said. "It says right here that if everyone in the United States recycled their Sunday newspapers, we could save 500,000 trees each week," said Mitch, breathing hard. "Then we'd have more trees and a greener earth. And if we saved our newspapers every day, we'd save millions of trees."

"That sounds important," said Dad.

"We can even recycle cereal boxes and envelopes and letters and all kinds of paper." Mitch looked up at his father as they walked to the car.

"And guess what else? Mr. Morgan said the paper four people use in one year weighs as much as a big car—maybe even a van like ours."

"I didn't know that," said Dad.

"I know," said Mitch. "Mr. Morgan said most people don't know stuff like that. He said we should share it with our moms and dads." Mitch pulled on his dad's jacket sleeve. "Could we start taking our paper to the recycling center?" he asked.

"Let's talk to your mother about it," said Dad, as they met Mother and Molly at the door. "It's a good idea. But it sounds like a lot of work. I'm not sure where we'd put all the paper we save. And we'd have to find a place to take it."

"No, we wouldn't," said Mitch, as he climbed into the van beside his sister, Molly. "He turned over the note in his hand. Here's a list of recycling places."

"What are you two up to?" asked Mother from the front seat.

Molly leaned over Mitch's shoulder. "I want to see too," she said.

Mitch told his mother and sister what he learned about saving paper.

Then he showed them the list.

"It sounds like a fine idea," said Mother. "But we couldn't start until next month. I'm too busy now with the children's choir to take on any new projects."

Mitch slumped back in his seat as Dad pulled out of the church parking lot. He felt sad. He was excited about being a paper-saver. But his mother and father didn't sound excited.

Then Mitch remembered something else Mr. Morgan had said. He had told Mitch and the other children to be polite when sharing with their parents. "Don't bug them," he had said. "If they don't help right away, do something yourself to show them how important it is."

Mitch wondered what he could do to show his mother and dad how important it is to recycle paper. Just then Dad pulled into their driveway. Mitch and Molly opened the door of the van and jumped down.

"One hour till lunch," said Dad. "I'm the cook today."

"Okay," said Mitch. He and Molly walked into the garage. Mitch had an idea. "Come here," Mitch whispered to his sister. "Do you want to help me make a place to save papers?"

"Sure," said Molly. "What should I do?"

Mitch pointed to a spot where some gardening tools stood against the wall. "We could clean up this corner," he said. "Stack the papers here." Mitch picked up the broom and began sweeping. "If Mom and Dad see us doing it, maybe they'll want to help too," he said. "And then maybe they'll drive us to the recycling center. I want to save the trees, don't you, Molly?"

"Sure I do," said Molly. "Hey, Mitch. Maybe we could use those big boxes to put the paper in," said Molly. She pointed to some empty boxes next to Dad's workbench.

"That's a great idea," said Mitch. "We need three boxes. We could make a sign for each one."

"One could say 'NEWSPAPER,' " said Molly. "What would the other ones say?"

"How about 'CARDBOARD' for one?" said Mitch. "We could put empty cereal boxes and other cardboard in there. And the other one could

say . . . " Mitch stopped for a minute to think. "Hey, I know. 'MIXED PAPER.' Mr. Morgan said envelopes and letters and school paper and computer paper are called mixed paper."

Mitch carried the boxes to the corner of the garage. He wanted to surprise his mother and dad, so he was very quiet. Then Mitch put the gardening tools on the other side of the garage. Molly ran into the house and came back with colored paper and marking pens. Mitch printed the signs. Molly taped them to the sides of the boxes.

Mitch heard Dad call them for lunch just as he finished cleaning. After eating, Mitch picked up the Sunday newspaper from the floor. "Dad, Mom, are you finished reading the paper?" asked Mitch.

"Yes, we are," said Mother.

"I want to look at the comics," said Mitch.

"Me too," said Molly.

Mitch and Molly looked at the comics together. Mitch read some of them out loud.

Then Mitch and Molly carried the paper out to the garage while Mother and Dad washed the lunch dishes.

"Molly, you look in the trash basket by the desk in the den," said Mitch. "Bring all the old envelopes and computer paper and letters you find. And be real quiet. We want to surprise Mom and Dad."

Mitch put the Sunday newspaper in the box marked "newspapers." Molly tip-toed into the house. A few minutes later Mitch heard her come back to the garage. She was holding a big bag full of paper and an empty cereal box.

"Over here, Molly," Mitch whispered. He pointed to the box marked "MIXED PAPER." "Dump the papers in here."

"I'll put the cereal box here," Molly said, touching the sign that said "CARDBOARD."

"Are we finished?" she asked.

"Almost," said Mitch. "But I have one more idea."

"What is it?" asked Molly.

"Let's go to Mrs. Bell's house. Maybe she'll give us her mixed paper and her newspapers."

"And maybe she has some old oatmeal boxes," said Molly. "She likes oatmeal for breakfast."

Mitch and Molly ran over to Mrs. Bell's house and rang the bell.

"Good morning," said Mrs. Bell as she opened the door. "Would you like to come in for some orange juice?" she asked.

"No thanks," said Mitch, hopping from one foot to the other. "We're in a big hurry. Molly and I are learning how to be paper-savers." Mitch saw Molly nod her head up and down. "If you're finished reading your Sunday paper, could we have it? We're helping save God's green earth by recycling newspapers and letters and envelopes and . . . "

Molly interrupted. "And cereal boxes," she said. "Do you have any empty oatmeal boxes?"

"Yes I do," said Mrs. Bell. "I put my knitting yarn in them. And sometimes I cover them with pretty paper and use them as gift boxes."

"You do?" asked Mitch. "Wow! Mr. Morgan said if we use empty boxes for saving stuff, or write on both sides of our paper, that's recycling too." Mitch waited on the front porch while Mrs. Bell got her newspaper and cereal boxes.

She came back with her arms full. "I'm happy to help," she said and handed the paper and boxes to Mitch and Molly. "Do you want me to keep saving my paper and boxes for you?"

"That would be great," said Mitch. "Thanks, Mrs. Bell. We'll come back next Sunday to pick them up."

Then Mitch got another idea. Maybe he and Molly could collect newspapers and mixed paper from their other neighbors. Mitch told Molly his idea. "Each family could take turns driving the paper to the recycling center."

Molly jumped up and down. Her red curls

flopped on her back. "Come on, Mitch. Let's go to the houses now," said Molly.

Mitch grabbed Molly by the sleeve of her pink dress. "Wait," he said. "We better tell Mom and Dad first." Just then Dad walked into the garage.

"It's awfully quiet in here," he said. "What have you two been doing?"

Before Mitch could answer, he saw his dad walk over to the clean corner. "Hey, this is great!" said Dad, smiling. He looked at each box and then called Mitch's mother.

"Look at this," said Dad. "Mitch and Molly have been working hard."

Mitch could feel his heart pound. He hoped his mother and dad would like what he and Molly had done. For a minute, he was scared they wouldn't let him use the old boxes. He was afraid they might be angry that he went over to Mrs. Bell's.

"Where did you get all this paper?" asked Dad.

"Who made these colorful signs?" asked Mother.

Mitch saw that his parents were smiling at him and Molly. They're not mad, Mitch thought.

"You two have been busy," said Dad. "I'm proud that you've collected so much paper. It would be very sad to throw it away." Then he winked at Mitch. "Say, Mitch, did you know that the paper four people use in a year weighs as much as our van?"

Mitch laughed. Maybe his dad wanted to become a paper-saver too.

"We could make this a neighborhood project," said Dad. "Mitch, how about sending some notes to all the neighbors? Maybe they'd like to save their paper too."

"Daddy, Mrs. Bell said she'd help." Molly pointed to the newspaper and cardboard in the big boxes. "Look, these are her oatmeal boxes, and this is her Sunday paper."

Dad put his hands on his hips. Then he

smiled at Mitch and Molly. "You two are ahead of me," he said.

"And guess what else, Daddy?" asked Molly.

"What's that, pumpkin?" he asked.

"Mitch said the moms and dads could take turns driving to the recycling center," said Molly, smiling.

"I like that idea," said Dad.

"If everyone took a turn," said Mother, "it wouldn't be too much work for us."

Mitch could hardly believe it. His mom sounded interested. "What about the children's choir?" asked Mitch. "You said you couldn't do anything more this month."

"I see how much you and Molly can do without my help," said Mother. "I can certainly take my turn driving to the recycling center."

"Wow! Thanks, Mom. Thanks, Dad," said Mitch. In his heart he whispered, Thanks, Lord. Suddenly Mitch felt peaceful inside. Molly

45

had helped him set up the corner in the garage and fix the boxes. His dad thought the idea was a good one. His mom would take a turn driving. They were all helping to save God's green earth.

Mr. Morgan was right, thought Mitch. We shouldn't bug our parents about recycling. We should just do something ourselves to *show* them how important it is.

SOMETHING YOU CAN DO TO SAVE GOD'S GREEN EARTH

Ask your parents if you can set up three boxes for saving paper. Make signs for each box: *Newspapers, Mixed Paper, Cardboard.* When the boxes are full, ask a parent or other adult to take them to the recycling center. Every time you save paper you will be saving God's trees. Make a newsletter that tells other kids at school or in your neighborhood about saving paper. You can suggest some ideas for them to follow.

Mitch and Molly, Bottle Bandits

Mitch heard his mother calling him from his sister's room. He ran to the door. Mother was sitting on the edge of Molly's bed. Molly was crying.

"What's wrong?" asked Mitch.

"Molly doesn't feel well," said Mother. "She has a sore throat and a runny nose. Would you please bring her a glass of orange juice?" Mother rested her hand on Molly's forehead. "I'm going to take her temperature. I might need to take her to the doctor."

"I'm sorry you're sick," said Mitch. He dashed out of Molly's room and down the stairs. Mitch poured a big glass of orange juice and brought it up to his sister. Molly was still crying when Mitch walked into her room.

"Why are you crying?" Mitch asked.

Mother answered for her. "She's sad because she wants to be a bottle bandit."

Mitch interrupted Mother. "What's that?"

Dad walked into the room as Mitch and Mother talked.

"Bottle bandits are kids who collect and recycle glass," said Dad. "Molly's teacher saw the name in a book on how to save the earth. She decided to use it for their class project."

Mother took down the note pinned to Molly's bulletin board. "This morning from 10:00 to 12:00 noon," she said, "the children and their parents will collect glass bottles and jars. They'll meet at the park afterwards for a picnic lunch."

"Some of the parents will take the glass to the recycling center," said Dad. "They will use the money they get to buy new library books for Molly's classroom."

Mother patted Molly's hand. "But Molly is just too sick to go out," she said.

"No I'm not," said Molly, folding her arms across her chest. "I'm not sick. I'm not sick," she yelled.

Mitch watched his mother fluff Molly's pillow. Then she tucked the quilt under Molly's chin and kissed her on the cheek. "Honey, I know you're disappointed," she said, "but you are sick. I can't let you go outside. I'll write a note to your teacher. Mitch can give it to her on Monday."

Mitch waved good-bye to Molly. He went back to his room. Molly sure was unhappy. He knew she really wanted to collect bottles with the other kids and their parents. I wish I could take her place, thought Mitch.

"Hey, wait a minute," he said out loud. "Maybe I can." Mitch remembered how Molly had helped him find a project for the science fair. This would be his chance to help her.

Mitch looked at his calendar as he walked out of his room. "Oh no," he said. "Today is Saturday. I'm supposed to go to Matt's for a video game and lunch." Mitch didn't want to give up his morning at his friend's house. But he also wanted to help Molly.

Just then the phone rang. Mitch answered. It was Matt. Mitch listened as Matt told him about his new video game and the great lunch his mother was making for them. Mini-pizzas, oatmeal cookies with raisins, and fruit punch were Mitch's favorites.

Maybe I could help Molly with some other project, thought Mitch. I don't want to miss going to Matt's. "See you, Matt," said Mitch. "I'll be at your house at 10:00." He hung up the phone.

Mitch walked by Molly's room. Molly was sleeping. Mother tip-toed out into the hall. "Let's be quiet," she said. "Molly needs a good rest."

Mother and Mitch walked downstairs to

the family room. "I feel sad this happened today," said Mother. "Molly was so excited about being a bottle bandit."

Mother sat down at her desk and took out a pad of paper and a pen. "Molly wanted to go on the picnic too. And she wanted the special bookmark that Mrs. Benton is passing out to all the kids who help."

Suddenly Mitch had a funny feeling in his stomach. He knew how important this was to Molly. But he didn't tell his mother because he didn't want her to keep him home from Matt's.

"We learned about recycling glass in science," said Mitch. "It sure is a good way to save the earth." Mitch kept talking. He hoped his mother wouldn't notice that he was nervous.

"Mom, did you know that every month people throw away enough glass bottles and jars to fill up a giant skyscraper? Like the Empire State Building in New York," said Mitch.

"That's a lot of glass," said Mother.

Then Mitch remembered something else he learned. "Mom, our teacher said people throw away 28 billion bottles and jars every year. That's really bad for the earth," he said.

Mother folded the note and put it into an envelope. "You're right," she said. "What do you think we could do about it?"

Mitch looked out the window. "We could think of some ways to save glass." Then he looked at the empty glass on the desk. "Hey, Mom, wait a minute. We could stop using so much glass," said Mitch, "like this one you use for your water. We could use plastic drinking cups. And we could stop buying juice in glass bottles."

Mother got up and walked into the kitchen. Mitch followed her. She picked up an empty apple juice bottle. "You know, Mitch, you're right. I never thought about that before. I could buy frozen juice and add water in a pitcher."

"That would save more glass," said Mitch.

"And we could save the glass bottles and jars we're finished with," said Mother. "We could take them to the recycling center when we take the newspapers."

"That's a great idea," said Mitch. Mother opened the pantry door. "Look at all these jars," she said. "I need to wash and save them when we're finished with them. I used to throw them in the trash. I don't want to do that anymore."

"Molly and I could fix a place to put them in," said Mitch.

"Like you did for the newspapers," said Mother.

Suddenly Mitch felt a little better. Here was another project he and his family could do to save God's green earth. Mitch looked at the clock. It was almost 10:00. He had to leave for Matt's house.

"Mom, I've got to go to Matt's now," said Mitch.

"I nearly forgot," said Mother. "I was so

worried about Molly." Mitch kissed his mother good-bye. She hugged him. "Have a good time and be careful. Remember, you're precious to me—and to Jesus," she said.

"Bye, Mom," said Mitch as he ran out the door.

As Mitch walked to Matt's house, he felt funny inside. He wanted to play the video game. And he wanted to eat lunch with his friend. But he also wanted to help Molly be a bottle bandit and get a special bookmark like the other kids.

As Mitch turned the corner he whispered a little prayer. "What should I do, God? I want to help Molly, but I want to play with Matt too."

Mitch could see Matt playing ball in the front yard of his house. He ran the rest of the way down the block. Mitch watched Matt and his brother toss the ball. Then he ran up to Matt and told him about Molly and the bottle bandits. "I want to play with you, Matt, but I want to help her too. I don't know what to do."

Matt dropped the ball and walked over to Mitch. "Remember what we learned in Sunday school? About doing stuff for other people the way you'd want them to do it for you?"

Mitch thought about that for a minute. He knew Matt was right, but he still wasn't sure what to do. Then Mitch thought about how Molly had helped him make boxes to recycle paper. And he remembered how she helped him with the garage sale.

"Hey, Matt, it feels like God is answering my prayer through you. I asked Him what to do. I think He wants me to take Molly's place." Then Mitch remembered how Mr. Morgan had said that sometimes God uses other people to answer our prayers.

Suddenly Mitch got a peaceful feeling inside. He knew the right thing to do. He would collect glass for Molly. He could play the video game some other time with Matt. Mitch ran in the house to find Matt's mother. He told her about Molly and the bottle bandits, and how God used Matt to give him the right answer.

Matt's mother smiled and ruffled his hair. "Thanks for telling me, Mitch," she said. "We'll invite you another time."

Just then Matt ran into the family room. "Mitch, I'll help you," he said. Matt's mother said that was a wonderful idea. The boys ran back to Mitch's house to tell his mom their surprise plan to collect bottles and jars for Molly.

"We'll go to all the houses on our block and Matt's," said Mitch. "We'll put two boxes in the wagon."

"Good," said Mother. "When you come back we'll put the boxes in our van and Dad will drive you to the park."

Mitch and Matt collected glass bottles and jars for two hours. Then they walked back to Mitch's house. They helped his father load the boxes into the van. Mother waved good-bye from Molly's window while Dad drove them to the park.

Dad parked the van near the picnic benches. Mitch hopped out of the van and ran over to Molly's teacher. "My sister Molly is sick," he said. "But my friend, Matt, and I took her place, if that's okay. We brought two boxes of glass bottles and jars for Molly."

"What a lovely thing to do," said Molly's teacher. "You must be hungry. I hope you can both stay for lunch." She looked at Mitch's father in the van. "Your father is welcome too."

"Thanks," said Mitch. "But my dad has to get home for Molly."

Mrs. Benton reached into a brown envelope. "Please take this special bookmark to Molly," she said. "Tell her thank you from all of us. We'll say a prayer for her to get well soon."

Then Mrs. Benton opened a white box on the picnic table. She handed Mitch three cupcakes. "I almost forgot. Here's a cranberry cupcake for her when she's well. And one each for you and your friend."

Mitch and Matt said good-bye and thank you to Mrs. Benton. Then they ran to the van. Mitch told his father what happened. They drove back to Mitch's house. Mitch and Matt jumped out of the van and dashed upstairs to Molly's room. She was sitting up in bed sipping orange juice. Mother was reading her a story.

Mitch walked up to Molly's bed. He kept his hands behind his back. "Molly, guess what I have for you?" he asked.

"What?" asked Molly.

"This." Mitch stuck out his right hand. "It's a bookmark from Mrs. Benton. It says, "Thanks for being a Bottle Bandit!"

Mitch watched Molly's blue eyes open wide. "Gosh, Mitch. How did you get that?"

Mitch turned to Matt, who was standing behind him. "Matt and I took your place," he said. "We collected bottles and jars in our neighborhood. We dropped them off at the park. Dad drove us."

Then Mitch remembered the cupcake. He opened the bag he was holding. "Molly, I almost forgot. Here's a cupcake for you when you get well."

Molly smiled the biggest smile Mitch had ever seen.

"Gee, thanks, Mitch. Thanks, Matt."

"Boys, you've done a great job," said Dad.

"How about if we keep on saving glass?" asked Mother. "Molly told me how recycling glass saves energy for making new glass." Then Mother pulled a science book off the bookshelf near Molly's bed. She pointed to a page of ideas on how to save energy. "When we recycle even one glass, we save enough energy to light a bulb for four hours."

"Like the one in the lamp on my dresser?" asked Molly.

"That's right," said Mother.

"We could save glass like we save paper," said Dad.

"Matt and I could fix a place in the garage,"

said Mitch.

"Go for it," said Dad.

Mitch and Matt ran out to the garage. They pulled two empty boxes off a shelf. Mitch printed the words *Clear Glass* on one box. "You print *Green Glass* on the other one," Mitch told Matt.

"Why do we need signs?" asked Matt. "Can't we put all the glass together?"

Mitch picked up a clear glass jar from his dad's workbench. Then he reached for an empty green soda bottle. "Mr. Bond said the recycling people like us to put the same color glass together," said Mitch. "Then they can make new glass out of the old pieces. They don't want to mix the colors."

Mitch and Matt finished their work. Then they set the boxes next to the ones for recycling paper. Just then Dad stood in the doorway.

"Telephone for you, Matt," he said.

Mitch and Matt ran into the house. Matt answered the phone. When he hung up he was smiling. "Mom invited you over to play my video game and have dinner," said Matt.

"Wow!" Mitch didn't know what else to say. God sure had blessed him. Today I helped Molly, he thought. I helped save God's green earth. I helped set up our own recycling boxes. And now I get to go to Matt's after all. "Thank You, God," said Mitch.

SOMETHING YOU CAN DO TO SAVE GOD'S GREEN EARTH

Ask your parents if you can save glass bottles and jars. Set up two boxes, one for clear glass and one for green glass. If you have other colored glass, make a box for each color. When the boxes are filled, ask your parents or other adults to take them to the recycling center. Ask your neighbors to save their glass for you. Tell them about separating the colors. Offer to make signs to go on their boxes. They can bring their full boxes to your house or take them directly to the recycling center.

Mitch and Molly
And the Clean Closets

Mitch looked at the calendar on the wall over his bed. Only five more days, he thought. Next Sunday is the Christmas toy collection at church for the homeless kids. Mitch opened his football bank and shook the money onto his bed. "Four quarters," he counted, "five dimes, one nickel, and three pennies."

Molly peered over his shoulder. "How much do you have?" she asked.

"Shh," said Mitch. "I'm still counting. One dollar and fifty cents," he said as he pushed the quarters and dimes into a little pile. Then he added the nickel and three pennies. "Gosh, that's only a dollar fifty-eight."

Maybe his sister would help him out. "Molly," he said, "I don't have enough money to buy a toy. And I sure don't have enough to buy Christmas presents for you and Mom and Dad."

Mitch knew Molly's Snow White bank was always full. "Can I borrow five dollars? I promise I'll pay you back," said Mitch.

Molly frowned and poked the carpet with the toe of her sneaker. "Mitch, you said that before, for Daddy's birthday. Remember?" She folded her arms across the stripes on her red and white shirt. Mitch could tell she was mad. "You didn't pay me back. You *still* owe me two quarters," said Molly. "And Daddy's birthday was last summer."

Girls sure can be a pain, thought Mitch. Especially sisters. "Gosh, Molly, we're in the same family. I'll pay you back, I promise."

"I need money for presents too," she said. "If I give you my money then I won't have any."

She's right, thought Mitch. But he didn't want to tell her she was right. "Okay, Molly, keep your old money. See if I care."

"You're not very nice," yelled Molly. "It's not my fault you don't have enough. You're supposed to keep your money in your bank, not take it out."

Mitch didn't want to hear any more. He already felt ashamed that he didn't save part of his allowance like Dad suggested. And he felt sad that he hadn't put any money in the collection plate at church for two weeks. Then Mitch remembered the Thanksgiving food baskets for poor families. He didn't have money for that either. And he sure didn't have enough to buy the new baseball trading cards he wanted.

Mitch didn't know what to do. He decided to ride his bike and think about it. As he walked out of his room, he saw the little sign on his closet door. Dad had put it there one day when Mitch was upset about a Little League game. It said, "Have you prayed about it?"

Dad had said it would help him remember to ask the Lord for help.

I sure do need help, thought Mitch. Dear God, he prayed, Dad says You're our heavenly Father. He said You'll help us whenever we need it. Well, I need help fast. I need money for the toy collection. Can You get me some right away? Thank You, Lord. Amen.

Mitch ran down the stairs and through the family room. Before he could get out the door he felt his mother grab him by the sleeve. "Hey, slow down, young man. Where are you going in such a hurry?"

"Uh, nowhere. I mean, I'm going outside to ride my bike," Mitch said with his head down.

"You seem sad," said his mother. "Is anything wrong?"

"I was just thinking about the toy collection at Sunday school next week. I want to buy a really neat toy for one of the homeless kids."

"That's very nice of you," said Mother.

"But Mom, I don't have enough money. Only a dollar and 58 cents." Mitch grabbed a handful of raisins and nuts from the bowl on the table. "Seems like my money disappears." Then Mitch remembered how he spent $1.00 on a plastic ring. It broke the first day he got it. And he bought some racing cars from his friend Matt for $2.00. But they didn't seem so great when he brought them home.

Mother interrupted Mitch's thoughts. "That sounds like a problem," she said. "But I'm sure you'll think of a way to earn more. If you need help, let me know. I can always put you to work," she said with a twinkle in her eye.

Mitch hated vacuuming, and he hated sweeping the garage. But if that was all he could do to make money, then okay, he'd do it.

Mother reached for her sweater and purse. "Molly and I are going to pick up Fluffy at the vet's," she said. "We'll be back in half an hour." She gave Mitch a hug. "Daddy's working in the yard." Mother turned toward the stairs. "Come on Molly, time to go."

Mitch nearly ran into his sister as he dashed up the stairs and she ran down. "Oh, Mitch," Mother called after him. "I nearly forgot. I want you and Molly to clean out your closets tonight. And I mean *really* clean them," she said. "Nick and Nancy are going to stay with us for a few days. Their mom and dad are going on a trip. We need room for their clothes and toys. This is a good time to get started."

Gosh, thought Mitch. They're just our cousins. Why do we have to clean for them? Mitch felt his face get hot. He was mad. Mad at Mom for making him clean, and mad at Molly for not loaning him the money.

Mitch said good-bye to Mother and Molly, then ran into his room. He opened his closet. He didn't like what he saw. The box with his baseball cards was bent at the corner. His football helmet was scratched. Books and shoes were in a pile on the floor. Broken toys and games lay on top of each other. Some of his shirts and pants had fallen off the hangers.

What a mess! "I don't have time now," shouted Mitch. "I've got to make some money for the toy collection."

But Mitch knew his mom wasn't kidding. If she said to clean the closet, she meant it. Mitch stood on his tiptoes and pulled out the box with his baseball cards. Suddenly books, games, and toys tumbled down all at once. Mitch plopped down on the carpet outside the closet. "Now what am I going to do?" he said, half crying. "I'll never get all this work done and earn the money too."

"What's all that noise up there?"

Mitch heard his dad's voice as his father came running up the stairs.

"I'm in here," said Mitch.

"Sounds like an earthquake," said Dad, laughing. "What's going on?"

Mitch told Dad about not having enough money for the toy collection. Then he told him about having to clean the closet. "How am I going to do all this in time for Christmas?" Mitch asked.

"Well, let's think about this," said Dad. "Hey, I have an idea. I saw this flier at work." Mitch's father pulled out a crumpled sheet of paper from his pocket. Mitch smoothed it out and read the large, printed words. "PASS IT ON, DON'T TOSS IT OUT." It had some other stuff about recycling too.

"Maybe you could pass on some of your toys and games instead of tossing them out," said Dad. "It would be good for the earth too." He picked up a box of small plastic cars. Mitch hadn't played with them in over a year.

"If we throw them in the garbage, they'll go into the ground," said Dad. "Our earth is already filled with trash. How about giving these cars to the toy collection?"

"All the kids are bringing *new* toys," said Mitch. He stood up and brushed off his pants. "Our teacher said it would be nice to give them something brand new with money we earned."

"I see," said Dad. "Well, let's think about this. There must be a way you can earn money, and still save God's earth from another mound of trash." He stood up and walked toward the door. "I'm going to fix some orange juice. I'm thirsty after all that yard work. Would you like a glass?"

"Wait a minute, Dad. I just thought of something." Mitch jumped up and opened the closet door. "Remember when Mrs. Bell had a garage sale? She made $200 in one day," said Mitch. "She said she didn't believe in tossing things out—especially when someone else could use them. Is that the same thing as passing it on?" asked Mitch. "You know, like it said on the flier?"

"Sure is," said Dad.

"Maybe Molly and I could have a garage sale for kids. We could sell our old toys and games, and some of the clothes we don't wear."

Mitch could feel himself getting excited. He

pulled out his Candy Land game. He never played with that anymore. Then he grabbed some books that he was finished with. Next, he found two coloring books and some colored pencils. Then he remembered his old scooter in the garage. And he picked up the little train he put together from a kit Grandpa had given him.

Mitch knew that Molly had a bunch of toys and clothes too. "Dad," said Mitch, as he piled all the toys and games together in the corner of his room. "Could we have a garage sale on Saturday? Molly and I could do it together. Then I'd have enough money to buy a toy for one of the homeless kids." Mitch tugged at his dad's sleeve. "Please, Dad. We'd have enough money for Christmas presents. Our closets would be clean for Nick and Nancy. And we'd save God's earth."

Dad ruffled Mitch's hair. "That sounds like a great idea. Let's talk to Mother and Molly about it when they get home."

Suddenly Mitch didn't feel mad anymore.

He felt happy inside. Just then the front door opened. Mother and Molly walked in. "Mitch, smell Fluffy," shouted Molly. "She had a bath."

Mitch buried his nose in the cat's soft fur. "Mmm, she does smell good. Molly, I have something real important to tell you. We're going to have a kids' garage sale on Saturday. Dad said we could."

Molly and Mother listened as Mitch and Dad told them their plan. That night after dinner, Mitch and Molly cleaned out their closets. "Look at all this stuff," said Molly. "We can make lots of money for Christmas."

Dad typed a flier on his computer. Then he made copies for Mitch and Molly to pass out to their friends.

Pass it on! Don't toss it out!
Garage Sale
for Kids
Mitch and Molly's House
Saturday
9:00 to 2:00

Mother put price tags on the clothes, toys, games, and books for sale. By Saturday morning, everything was ready. Mother even made lemonade to serve to the shoppers. Mitch was so excited at breakfast, he could only eat a small bowl of oatmeal.

At five minutes to nine Mitch looked outside. "Wow, look at that. The kids are lined up down to the street." Mother and Dad and Molly looked out the window too.

"Mitch, you have a great idea. Looks like the whole neighborhood thinks so," said Dad.

Mitch and Molly and Mother and Dad started the sale at 9:00 sharp. For the next five hours, Mitch and Molly sold toys and games and books. Mother served lemonade. Dad collected the money. Fluffy slept in the driveway. By 2:00 in the afternoon, Mitch was so tired he could hardly walk. Molly and Mother and Dad looked tired too. They were sitting on a blanket sipping lemonade.

Mitch looked at the empty tables. He and Molly had sold almost everything. Mrs. Bell bought the scooter and plastic cars for her grandson. Sara and Nathan down the street bought the Candy Land game. The Wilson family bought all the used books.

Mitch counted the money again. All the quarters and dimes and nickels and pennies added up to $52.80. "Wow!" said Mitch. Dad helped Mitch divide the money into two piles. "That's $26.40 for Molly and $26.40 for me."

That evening Mitch lay in bed thinking about the good day he had had. It was nice to have the money he needed. But it was even nicer to think about all the good things he would do with it. First, he would buy a neat toy for one of the homeless children. Next, he would put money in the collection plate at church. Then, he would put some money in his football bank—and leave it there. He would also buy some new baseball trading cards.

Then suddenly Mitch thought of something really important. He jumped out of bed. He opened the box of money on his table and scooped up two of the coins. Then he tiptoed down the hall to Molly's room. He slid two quarters under her door and whispered through the crack. "Thanks, Molly. You're a neat sister."

Then Mitch ran back to his room and jumped into bed. He pulled the quilt around his neck. Before he drifted off to sleep he closed his eyes and whispered, "Thanks, Lord, for showing me what to do."

SOMETHING YOU CAN DO TO SAVE GOD'S GREEN EARTH

Clean your closet. Make three piles: used clothes, used toys, used games. Have a kids' garage sale like Mitch and Molly's. Share some of the money you earn with a homeless shelter, or a church mission, or other group. Ask your parents to help you choose. Spend some of the money on a gift for yourself. Save some in your bank.